ISBN:1-563-15-200-2

Paperback
© Copyright 1999 Janice N. Chapman
All rights reserved
First Printing —1999
Library of Congress # 98-88774

Request for information should be addressed to:

SterlingHouse Publisher, Inc.
The Sterling Building
440 Friday Road
Department T-101
Pittsburgh, PA 15209

Cover Art: Michelle Vennare - SterlingHouse Publisher
Typesetting: Pam Muzoleski

All rights reserved. No part of this publication may be reproduced, stored in a retrieval system, or transmitted in any form or by any means—electronic, mechanical, photocopy, recording or any other, except for brief quotations in printed reviews—without prior permission from the publisher.

This is a work of fiction. Names, characters, places, and incidents either are the product of the author's imagination or are used fictitiously. Any resemblance to actual events or persons, living or dead is entirely coincidental.

Printed in Canada

HELLO

OUT

THERE . . . !

Hello! . . . Hello out there . . .!

*To those of you who've come to share
the words that I now quote to you
and hope that you will enjoy them, too.*

By Janice N. Chapman

Contents

I. Humor
1. Hello Out There — 5
2. My Most Embarrassing Moment — 6
3. On Firing a Gun — 7
4. 'Twas a Dream — 8
5. The Croissants — 9
6. The Potato Chips — 10
7. The Mice — 11
8. Feeding Plants — 12
9. We Don't Have Motorcycles in Heaven — 13
10. P.S. — 14

II. Remembrance
1. The Class of 1959 — 16
2. The Razor Strap — 17
3. My Daughter, The Graduate — 18
4. When the War Was Won — 19
5. O Parachute — 20
6. The Razorback Hog — 21
7. The Stallion — 22
8. My Best Buddies — 23
9. Cycle Thirty-Two — 24
10. Miracle of Christmas — 25
11. How Lucky I have Been — 26
12. Anytown, U.S.A. — 27

III. Human Interest
1. If I Could Catch a Sunbeam — 30
2. Job Applications — 31
3. Be Nice to This Old Lady — 32
4. Miz Evelyn — 33
5. Can You Make a Dream Come True — 34
6. Living Up to a Child's Expectations — 36

7.	The Penny	37
8.	Money Doesn't Grow on Trees	39
9.	The Man Who Owns the Rocking 9	40
10.	The Shadowy Hand of Death	42
11.	Does God have a Credit Plan?	43
12.	If the Lord Should Come	45

IV. Nature

1.	The Silent Hills	47
2.	A Winter's Day	48
3.	The El Nino Children	49
4.	Hell's Highway	50
5.	The Glaciers	51
6.	A Farmer's Wife	52
7.	I'm a Meat and Potatoes Man	53
8.	Grandpa's Garden	54
9.	The Soil	56
10.	The Drought	57
11.	Nature Things	58

V. Love

1.	It Couldn't Be	60
2.	One Heart for Sale	61
3.	Eight Track Tape	62
4.	Your Game of Hearts	64
5.	The Man for Whom She Cries	65
6.	Uncle Sam's G.I.	67
7.	Love Library	69
8.	Old Souvenirs	70
9.	The Angel Was Crying	71
10.	Thank You for Sharing My Life	72

Hello Out There

Hello!... Hello out there...!
to those of you who've come to share
the words that I now quote to you,
and hope that you will enjoy them, too.
I warmly invite you to listen in
and eagerly await where I begin...
with lines so chosen for you to hear
that you, too, might hold them dear.
I'll understand if during my quote
I should hear murmurs about what I wrote.
And should I see a tear or two,
well...I'll try to understand that, too.
And if a chuckle should commence,
I'll read on in self-defense,
for I am not an orator...
but scared to death upon this floor!

Hello Out There

My Most Embarrassing Moment

My most embarrassing moment,
— and I can remember it yet! —
came while wearing to the prom
a "can-can" underskirt
that was made of nylon net.

If you've ever worn a "can-can",
then you know when I sat down,
that petticoat commenced to lift
the skirt of my evening gown.

For "can-can's" were designed
to cause the skirts of the gowns to flair.
But never was there one designed
to accommodate sitting in a chair.

And then you must consider,
that back in my era of time,
young girls didn't show their petticoats,
to do so was a crime.

So needless to say when I sat down,
my mother accosted me —
and right in front of my whole class
she gave me the third degree.

On Firing a Gun

Firing a gun has never been my thing.
Since it's all in fun, I'll give it a fling.
Put a shell in the chamber,
and it's ready to go.

Bring it up to the shoulder,
and sight it in slow.
Get a steady grip,
and aim with the eye.

Look through the scope
and pretend I'm a spy!
Pull the trigger at my own will,
and shoot at a target standing still.

Missed it by a country mile. . .
and laughter followed while
I picked myself up from the ground;
ejected from the gun the spent round.

I tried to figure out something to say
in self defense but in a joking way.
Heard the laughter begin to grow.
But I'm not a bad shot, you know.

It is just that the target
caught a puff of wind.
Stand back! I'll show you!
I'll do it again.

Hello Out There

'Twas a Dream

'Tis so real a thing it 'twould seem it 'twas not a dream, that boat and me tossed so free whilst upon The Emporium Sea.

Whilst the gale that swiped the sail bound me fearfully against the rail.

'Twas then with tear dimmed eyes, and much surprise, I saw the Sperm Whale rise.

All doubts forsook, by hook and crook, I knew him by the biology book.

Surprised by me, as I by he, he sank again into the Emporium Sea.

Could I have photographed the sea riff-raff, I'm sure 'twould made you laugh.

For it did me as I tossed so free upon the waves of the Emporium Sea.

As time wore on, and fears were donned, and surprise more calmly drawn upon,

I enjoyed thee, as they enjoyed me, whilst I tossed upon the Emporium Sea.

The Croissants

I was enjoying my lunch today
until my croissants got up to play.
They stood on end — that silly pair!
and danced upon the table where,
they scattered crumbs from their crust hold
as they bumped into my salad bowl.
They bumped into my glass of tea,
And it threatened to spill right down on me.
Those croissants dipped and swayed and swooned.
Scattered knife, and fork, and spoon.
Even on my cake, so danced this pair,
and across their own plate, now cold and bare.
My appetite drastically subsided
as onto my plate they danced and glided.
I almost had them in my grasp,
when they both bowed and turned and laughed.
This cannot be happening to me. . .
Quickly! Someone tell me this is fantasy!

Hello Out There

The Potato Chips

The potato chips decided
They'd all go get a tan.
When, asked one of the group,
"Are you sure we can?"

"Sure! The grease is boiling!"
came the reply from all the clan.
"All we have to do, old chip,
is jump into the pan!"

To the pan their pale selves marched,
and in they splattered, one by one.
Into the boiling liquid,
and basked there until they were done.

"Ah!" said one potato chip,
"I'm crispy since my fry."
And all the clan agreed with it,
for all were tanned and dry.

"All we need right now,"
declared another potato chip,
"Is to find and fall into
Our favorite brand of dip!"

The Mice

I overheard a conversation
between a pair of mice,
as they discussed the cheeses
Laying upon the counter sliced.

"I like the Swiss Cheese,"
said the shorter of the pair.
And he pointed to the one with holes,
and he did it with a flair.

"It looks almost like butter,
and you have to melt it down,
or else you'll get cheated —
especially if you eat it by the pound."

"Me, I like the cheddar cheese,"
The taller mouse declared.
And in their conversation,
not even the Monterey was spared.

But the short mouse still liked
the Swiss cheese, even with all its holes,
and the taller mouse could not change
the mind of that brazen little soul.

Feeding Plants

*Can you imagine how a plant
might curl its leaves to hold a knife or fork?
And then say something to you like —
"Won't you please pass the pork?"*

*Could you cope with a morning
when you looked out through the haze,
and found your lovely plants and shrubs,
like cattle, had gotten up to graze?*

*Well, you feed plants in the mornings.
That's what all the experts say.
And I just cannot help it
that my imagination came out to play.*

We Don't Have Motorcycles In Heaven

*I can tell you now
it was quite a fright. . .
I dreamed I had crashed
and gone to Heaven last night.
The Lord gave me a smile
and He held out His hand. . .
I shook it and told Him,
"I can't stay around here, man."
The Lord said, "But now
your spirit is free,
and you might as well
spend some time here with me."
"But I'm a working person
and I have to get back."
But He said, "Hang around here
and I'll take care of that.
Your body doesn't need you
now that you're here with me,
and there's only one problem
that I can foresee. . .
That bike of yours
will just have to go. . .
We don't have motorcycles
here in Heaven, you know."*

Hello Out There

P.S.:

I wrote you a letter and I mailed it to you.
On the bottom I signed it -P.S.: I love you.
You answered that letter like I knew you'd do;
and you signed it -P.S.: I'm sorry about you.

So I wrote you another to console your regret,
and I signed it -P.S.: I love you yet.
And the one you wrote me was rude, you know,
you signed it -P.S.: You know where you can go!

But I didn't have a way to get out there to you,
so I signed the next letter -P.S.: You're making me blue.
And you didn't help with your instant reply,
you signed it -P.S.: Take a kite and go fly.

Now how can I fly like a bird on the wing?
I signed the next one -P.S.: To me you're everything.
And the letter you sent made me kind of mad,
you signed it -P.S.: Now ain't that too bad?

But I forgave you this thing you had done,
and I wrote you -P.S.: My love you have won.
You said I must have been blind as a bat,
and signed it -P.S.: I'm sorry about that!

And since you were sorry for insulting me,
I signed the next -P.S.: Will you marry me?
And I couldn't believe the last letter from you,
you signed it -P.S.: My darling, we're through.

Remembrance

Hello Out There

The Class of 1959

Laverne, I know you knew us all,
who pranced your high school's herod halls.
In nineteen fifty-nine we knew,
we'd change the world, we Okie few.
Armed with goals, we Tiger fans
graduated with a wealth of plans.
Our motto, "Hitch Your Wagon to a Star"
would guide us long and guide us far.
Bathed in eagerness of unlike kind...
marched forth the class of 1959.
Where, like most other teens,
we hung our futures on our dreams.
How successful have you been,
my classmates from away back then?
Has your wagon of dreams come true?
Has your star been good to you?
A star, I've found my destiny...
among the authors of poetry.
And among treasured memories of mine,
the class of 1959

The Razor Strap

When Pop took you out behind the barn,
To talk to you — it certainly was not!
And you knew with each lick he gave,
you deserved just what you got.

There was no asking questions
of what you thought he should do.
When you did wrong, you already knew—
Pop's razor strap would straighten the bad in you.

That razor strap hung on the kitchen door;
a reminder to those who went and came.
It didn't matter what your gender was —
That strap treated you all the same!

Its little holes left their imprints
on the place where you sat down.
And reminded you it should be awhile
before the next time you decided to clown.

We didn't talk back to our folks back then.
We showed them respect in its full measure.
Otherwise, we knew full well where
that strap would take its pleasure.

We knew back then while we grew up,
our folks would take no crap.
And we grew up quite respecting. . .
Those trips behind the barn, and Pop's old razor strap.

Hello Out There

My Daughter, the Graduate

*The cap sat squarely upon her head,
the gown flowed long and gray.
A smile played upon her face. . .
This was graduation day!
Mom and the kids were there,
and for that she was glad.
It gave a bit more meaning
to the fact that she was about to be a grad.*

*The ceremonies took place
on Fort Benning at Marshall Hall,
and to give the presentation. . .
a four-star general received the call.
One by one they marched
up to the graduation stand,
where they received their diplomas
and shook the post commander's hand.*

*All were very proud of her
who made this graduating hike.
Congratulatory comments were made
by family and friends alike.
Photographs were taken
for the album she'll retain
of this endearing evening
that followed years of study and strain.*

*Later we asked, and they were honored,
To have their pictures made with her, too.
There were fours stars upon one's shoulders,
upon the other's there were two.
A moment she can cherish. . .
and a historic moment for the clan.
For she's the only one of the family who has held
a diploma in one, and generals in the other hand.*

When The War Was Won

*So vivid were the stories my grandfather told,
as his gentle voice made the war to unfold;
with fear for a companion, and hunger at his side,
and an enemy sniper his sometimes guide.*

*He told of the miles he'd walked in the cold;
in the mud and the rain they'd dug fox holes.
The shelling overhead was a thunderous roar. . .
along with the bullets finding places to score.*

*It was almost as though I was there. . .
as Granddad recounted the back roads where
the dead, the dying, and the countless maimed
had shed their blood, with the war to blame.*

*He spoke of various types of disease
that ran through the worn out troops with ease.
His gentle voice quivered a time or two,
and it seemed to accent the truths he knew.*

*I thought I might have seen a tear in his eye
as he murmured he still doesn't understand why,
with the thunder of war, and the horrifying cries,
the bullets had missed him and hit the other guys.*

*I flinched inside when he called my name,
and it seemed he bowed his head, as if in shame,
as he assured me he'd come home one lucky son. . .
because some hadn't made it when the war was won.*

Hello Out There

O Parachute

One thousand feet above the earth,
O Parachute, for what it's worth,
don't streamer on me lest I die,
For that would make my mother cry.

Up here in this cloud dotted blue,
we're all we have, me and you.
I must depend on your suspension lines
that have set me down a dozen times.

O Parachute, you must bear me out.
Forgive me if I have a doubt.
But carelessness cannot come to play
on this our destined jumping day.

And there's only seconds to the ground,
once you and I are airborne bound.
Every trip is one more test.
O Parachute, we must be the best.

The Razorback Hog

The old man's name was Larry,
and he liked to talk a lot.
And every now and then he'd tell
about the hog that put him in a spot.

He loved to hunt the old razorbacks.
He hunted them just for fun,
until he ran across the one
that cost him a leg and his new gun.

He claims he never heard the hog
that slipped up on him from behind.
He could only beat it off with his gun,
until a tree he could find to climb.

And as he dropped the gun
to climb into the tree,
The razorback ripped his left leg
from his ankle to his knee.

Some hours later the hog got bored
and finally let Larry alone,
where he could come down from the tree
and drag his injured body home.

He doesn't hunt the razor backs
like he used to, just for fun.
He thinks about it now and then,
then he remembers. . .what that last hog done.

Hello Out There

The Stallion

I watched as against the late sunrise
he reared and shook his stately head,
and bugled across the valley below
before rejoining the band of mares he led.
And all I could do was stand and stare.
In the morning sunrise he was a sight to behold.
I wanted that stallion with an awful desire.
I followed that horse long mile after mile,
completely consumed by my wanton desire.
I figured that he'd get tired after awhile,
and he figured the same thing about me,
as onward we traveled. . .mile after mile.
We traveled for days across grassy land,
and I can just see that stallion smile!
I swear I knew that horse had a plan.
He'd stop and turn to see if I was there,
or he'd come back and see how far he'd left me behind,
or he'd come back and just stand and stare.
He was playing with my mind.
Then he stole into my camp late one night,
like the Devil himself he tore up my camp,
drove off my trail horse and woke me with a fright.
He was a thunderous bolt of golden scamp!
He wanted to make sure I quivered in my bed.
He snorted and stamped and his nostrils flared,
and up and down he tossed his beautiful head.
But then he backed off with a "hee-hee-hee!"
And I knew I'd been beaten. . . and so did he.

My Best Buddies

My thoughts went back into the past
where my best buddy was my horse,
and not to be left out —
an old mangy dog, of course.

I could talk to my horse, Champion:
Tell him things I needed to talk about,
and he'd put his head around me,
and hug me to him: his way of loving me, no doubt.

And the dog, old Bozo, he'd wag his tail,
as though he understood every emotion.
and I never knew if he approved or disapproved
my every idea and notion.

If my horse could talk, boy, could he tell tales!
And if the dog could talk, too,
I might get thrashed soundly
for some of the things we three used to do.

They knew my every secret inside out,
and they hung onto my every word,
every tidbit of gossip I told them,
no matter how absurd.

And when I was crying or feeling low,
my best buddies were right there,
with horse hugs and puppy dog kisses,
to let me know they cared.

Hello Out There

Cycle Thirty-two

*My lights were all out
and you thought I was asleep,
When you pulled Thirty-two
into the drive across the street.
Twenty-nine cycles you have
built and named for me,
Since our parents first told us
our love couldn't be.
I never did know where
Number Thirty came from,
or what ever happened
To Cycle Thirty-one.
The years have been many,
and the times have been few,
that I've had a glimpse
of your cycles or you.
And when your voice told me
you were there across the street,
I went to my window,
and I had myself a peek.
I was looking at a ghost
of a man I once knew,
and a honey of a machine
You called the Cycle Thirty-two.
And then you were gone
with an echo from the past,
"If anything should happen to her,
get ahold of me fast."
So wherever you have gone,
and whatever you may do,
may the Lord ride with you
and the Cycle Thirty-two.*

Miracle of Christmas

I came home from work
with aching limb and bone,
and listened while our neighbor explained
the situation in their home.
Pre-Christmas had seen their Mother ill,
and their dad laid of as well.
Strife upon this Christmas Eve
upon their house had fell.
There would be no gifts this year,
nor would there be a tree.
For his wife's illness and him laid off
had left them in poverty.
But then his little girl,
the youngest there of four,
and she was not but nine in years —
well, perhaps a few days more,
came around to me,
and with a heart to so pure and true,
held up her little hands and said,
"Here, I picked this for you!"
A miracle of Christmas
I knew came from God above,
as I took from her the flower
she had picked and gave with love.
And as I hugged her to me
and gave this child a kiss,
I knew she could not have given
a greater gift than this.

Hello Out There

How Lucky I Have Been

How lucky I have been
that I could live in time,
where people cared for others,
and there was no selfish "mine."

Where a person's word
and a handshake a worthy note.
Trust the bond one carried proudly,
for it needed no legal note.

How lucky I have been
that I was taught the way,
to share in other people's needs
and to kneel with them to pray.

When a "thank you" was full payment
for whatever deeds were rendered there,
by respectful friends and neighbors
who took the time to care.

Janice N. Chapman

Anytown, U.S.A.

*I'm sitting and thinking about the places I've been,
and of the things that I've tried and never could win.
Of the persons I've met, and then forgotten about,
in the whirlwind of worry and loneliness and doubt.*

*I never did know there were things in this life
that could bring peace of mind without worry or strife.
I grew up in the country and around a small town,
where life was a turmoil and one big battleground.*

*One neighbor was your enemy, and the next was your
friend, and the next one down the line was apt to be
your kin. Where the local newspaper was outdone all
the time, by the parties that listened in on the telephone
line.*

*It was the best underground system the world's ever
had, because you listened to the good, and you listened
to the bad. They didn't need a telescope, or a
government spy, because everybody knew everybody's
business, and everybody knew why.*

*There was very little trust running through anyone's
veins, because fighting and rebellion was the
way they were all trained.
Where the children did things they knew they
shouldn't do, because they had found out their parents
were doing it, too.*

*Where the poor men's truth could never shine through,
because they got the blame for what the rich men'd do.*

Hello Out There

*They bore the burden of the high society abuse, and
with their own reputations paid the rich men's dues.*

*Where the rich man's money could sway the rule of the
court, and he could pat himself on the back and call
himself Sport. And his son could count on his daddy
every time, to get him off again to commit another petty
crime.*

*Where the deacon of the Church prayed for justice and
its lack, then turned right around and stole the shirt off
your back. Where there wasn't a fight that ever was
won,
without the threat of a knife or a gun.*

*Where the bitterness and hate mix with the bad and the
good, and the little child is robbed of his own childhood. And I never did know until I had moved away,
there are pleasanter things in this world of ours today.*

*Where a man can shed his worries and his blues,
and stand straight and tall in his own pair of shoes,
and look at the world with a fresh point of view,
and almost forget the past troubles he knew.*

*Where he can carry on a new fight in his own way,
To try to better the bad in Anytown, U.S.A..
Where he can hold his wife in a tender caress,
And know in his heart how well he's been blessed..*

Human Interest

If I Could Catch a Sunbeam

*If I could catch a sunbeam,
and hold it in my hand,
I wonder just how far
the ray from it would expand.
Would it expand from sea to sea,
and all across the land?
Would it be a light of warmth
that covets every man?
Would it brighten dark pathways
as it beamed across the earth?
If I could catch a sunbeam
how much would it be worth?*

Job Applications

*I wonder how many job applications
have I filled out by now?
It doesn't matter that they don't know me —
they could have hired me anyhow.*

*They claim they need the help —
and a job wouldn't hurt my feelings none.
But by the time I get the ap filled out,
they claim they've done hired someone.*

*Now, why don't I believe them
when they tell me those kind of things?
Why does it have a funky feeling,
and to my ears falsely ring?*

*They might say they don't want me
because I came in from another state,
and because I'm new and they don't know me,
that I'll just have to wait.*

*But if help is what they're needing —
and the job I have applied for —
Why is it they keep showing me —
The way to their front door?*

Be Nice to This Old Lady

*Be nice to this old lady
as I come stumbling by.
For there will come a day
you'll be as old as I.*

*There will be a day
when a smile will be a treasure.
And just a few kind words
will be your daily measure.*

*There will be a distant day
when youthful beauty will subside,
and then will be replaced
with age and wrinkles we can't hide.*

*Though surgery does do wonders
to help some of us to lie,
just favor me with a few kind words
as I come toddling by.*

*For no matter what configuration
within the boundaries of your skin lie,
be nice to this old lady —
One day it will be you instead of I.*

Miz Evelyn

*You never know what Miz Evelyn might say
during the course of our working day.
Some of the things her mouth will spit,
you wouldn't expect to come out of it.*

*Young and old, we love her all,
and some of us wish we had her call,
to keep us laughing from time to time,
with words that come from her witty mind.*

*But whether we're laughing, or if we fuss,
Miz Evelyn can hold her own with us.
And you never know what Miz Evelyn might say,
but we all love her, each in our own way.*

Hello Out There

Can You Make a Dream Come True?

Mama, can you make a dream come true?
Mama, let me tell my dream to you.
Last night I dreamed that we were rich, you see,
and that we'd forgotten about our poverty.

We forgot all those hand-me-downs,
and we forgot to live by charity.
and I wore the kind of clothes, Mama,
you can't afford to buy for me.

We forgot about all of our debts,
and that we ever owed a cent.
And we didn't have to worry
about having enough to pay the rent.

I dreamed we lived in a mansion
with carpets on all the floors,
instead of in this lowly shack
with its broken windows and sagging doors.

And out there in our driveway,
there sat a great big car —
The kind we can't afford, Mama,
as hard up as we are.

We had beautiful new furniture,
instead of someone else's oddities.
And we forgot what it was like
to stand in line for our commodities.

*We forgot to wait for our welfare check
that means so much to me and you,
and the social worker became someone
we forgot we ever knew.*

*In the dream we had everything
that worldly deeds can buy.
And we were well thought of by society —
Oh! We were living high!*

*And we forgot about all those days
when we couldn't afford a thing,
and felt that we were lucky
just to be considered as human beings.*

*We didn't have to feel guilty
about feeling out of place.
And folks didn't look down upon us —
Like we were so much human trash.*

*I know it was just a dream, Mama,
one I wish we were living through.
So, tell me, won't you, Mama,
Can you make a dream come true?*

Hello Out There

Living Up to a Child's Expectations

Living up to a child's expectations
is sometimes hard to do.
They build up a pedestal —
and that's where they put you.

They think moms and dads know everything.
They're idolized in every way
by those capable young fans
who live with them day to day.

They think their parents know the answer
to any questions they might ask.
They can really put you on the spot. . .
Coming up with answers is sometimes quite a task.

An answer you must come up with,
its wisdom to pass on to them,
because they're looking up at you
with that impish innocent grin.

They're expecting you to know the answer,
and pass onto them the truth.
While they gaze up at you expectantly
in the eagerness of youth.

And you know you cannot let them down,
no matter what prompts your answer's creation,
for one day they will stand the task —
of living up to a child's expectations.

Janice N. Chapman

The Penny

*There isn't too much that a penny will buy
with the everyday prices rising so high.
And one little penny may not make a dent
in the feel of your pocket — until after it's spent.*

*It could be you may not realize it's there,
if you happen to be a person with money to spare.
But how many dollars could you account for today,
had you taken and thrown all those pennies away?*

*And look at the taxes those pennies still pay
on the things that we go out and buy every day.
I suppose you might say the penny is a slave
to all the other coins that we choose to save.*

*When you're a person whose pockets are bare,
that's when you notice when the penny's not there!
That little red cent can look mighty darn big,
when it's something you don't have, and something you need.*

*It can make the difference in the things we can buy,
and for the lack of it we sometimes could cry.
Oh, try paying your rent with a penny not there. . .
and tell me you have a landlord who don't care!*

*Whether it's something to wear, or something to eat,
or something to sit in and rest your weary feet —
Something to enjoy, or something you need,
that little red cent can sure bring out your greed.*

Hello Out There

If you ever try living your life as a charity case,
you'll find that a penny has a mighty big face.
It's the hardest working coin that's made from the mint,
and still there's not much you can buy with a cent.

There are people wearing rags and their tables are
bare, on account of the penny that just wasn't there.
There's mansions that might have been standing today,
if it weren't for the pennies that stood in the way.

If you can live life without pennies, that's fine.
I wish I could say the same thing about mine.
But if you think I'm lying, then vanish your doubt —
and name me the places where a penny doesn't count.

Money Doesn't Grow on Trees

They say money doesn't grow on trees.
But if it does, I'd like to know where.
And believe me when I say —
I'd like to own some acreage there!

Can you imagine a garden grown
in rows of trees of currencies?
Or to look down straight rows
of silver coin? Or copper pennies?

Can you imagine picking
from your own plants and trees,
just simply the amount of money
you think you're going to need?

But then they just might be
like the annuals that come and go.
One might have to harvest coin in season,
if we could our money grow.

Perhaps we'd learn to budget better,
and save more of our money, too.
if all we had to depend on —
was the money that we grew!

Hello Out There

The Man Who Owns The Rocking 9

Every time that I went home again
I'd hear tales of their favorite son.
Folks were quick to tell me
how they're proud of what he's done!

But when I asked to meet him,
I found that I had sinned:
For I'm a married woman,
and he has a girlfriend.

No matter who I asked to meet him,
they'd just point him out...
"That's him over there!"
To me they'd all but shout.

No rights did I have...
just visiting as it were...
To create such a scandal!
To cause their town such a stir!

Protection must be afforded
to their favorite brat. —
No married woman would corrupt him;
the town would see to that!

Maybe it's the city in me
that mis-understood their clout,
but to introduce me to him —
not a one was just about!

*Then as we walked into the restaurant,
my sister walked on to his booth,
and I did something UN-lady like...
I did something real uncouth.*

*I walked over to where she stood,
engaged in chatting with the man,
I said, "You must be Jerry!"
And I told him my name is Jan.*

*A rancher and a cattle man,
and yet the poem he pens.
And publishes them himself, he does,
for the locals and his friends.*

*The eve of my departure,
he stopped in for awhile.
We scanned each other's verse
and parted with a smile.*

*We discovered we had grown up
not too many miles apart.
And while our styles are different,
our poetry is our art.*

*Now the shroud of mystery
has been lifted from my mind.
And I've finally met the man
who owns the Rocking 9.*

The Shadowy Hand of Death

When the shadowy hand of death
cradles the living soul,
and a two-by-six opening
becomes the body's goal,
who then will shed a tear
in past remembrance
of the one who lies in the casket
in his or her eternal trance?
Who will then lament upon
past deeds the dead has done,
or commentate about
the successes the deceased has won?
Though his memory be legend
among his relatives and some he knew,
shortly will he be remembered
when his life on earth is through.

Does God Have a Credit Plan?

*Oh, tell me now does Heaven
operate on installment plans?
Because I can't help but wonder,
does God have a credit plan?*

*For as long as I can remember
everything that I have owned,
has been bought on some kind
of a long term credit loan.*

*I'm bogged down with creditors,
and bills I can hardly pay —
How would I get into Heaven
if I were to die today?*

*When a person is as poor
a person as I am —
will the Master Charge card
help him in on Heaven's plan?*

*Does Saint Peter have a special line
that we'll stand in up there,
while we await a credit plan
before we climb those golden stairs?*

*Is there some kind of labor force
beyond those pearly gates,
where we can all work out
our long-term credit fates?*

Hello Out There

*In the land where the trials
and the troubles are to be no more,
can you tell me how does God
compensate the underpaid and the poor?*

*Will He tell us we're not fit
to walk on Heaven's shores:
That our credit isn't good enough
to pass through Heaven's door?*

*And I wonder what kind of interest
will we have to pay up there. . .
When God becomes our creditor
on our Heavenly fan-fare?*

If The Lord Should Come

I don't know just what I'd do if I should have the fate,
to look out some fine morning and see the Lord come
through my gate.

I don't know if I could invite Him right on in, and give
Him a cup of coffee and ask Him how He'd been,
because it might be on a day my house is in a mess,
and I may not have even bothered to get dressed.

And, if I should have to ask, He wouldn't take it so kind,
Lord, could you leave for now, and come back another
time?
It might justly embarrass me if I should have to sin,
and think up some quick excuse that I could
give to Him.
Or tell Him I was sorry that today He'd
chosen to come.
Why, He never would forgive me the sins that I have
done!

Still, I might be feeling fine and ask Him right on in,
and tell Him I'd rejoice any time He could come again.
It might be on a day I'd jump and shout with glee,
and tell Him I was thankful He had the time to spare for
me.

Hello Out There

Nature

The Silent Hills

They gave my heart many joyous thrills,
those ever beckoning, silent hills.
While down below, yet safe and sound,
the canyons cut into the ground.
And ever so narrow, or deep and wide,
Breathtaking valleys choose to hide.
The little streams flowing freely, too,
blend their color with Heaven's blue.
And the beauty of the setting sun,
when at last the day is done,
casting shadows along the mountain's might,
is at best a stunning sight.
And with the coming of the dawn,
you'll find feeding, both doe and fawn.
And hear the singing of the morning fowl
as Nature's own begin to prowl.
Then you'll see the morning fog
that blankets the quiet mountain dialog.
And then, my friend, while you're still there,
you'll breathe deeply of the mountain air.
And the sun shall rise again,
releasing the beauty remaining within,
the grasp of grandeur that is ever instilled
in those ever-beckoning, silent hills.

Hello Out There

A Winter's Day

So fresh the air with its morning chill,
and the wind itself today is still.
And mounding up in glistening glow,
the freshly fallen drifted snow.

Icicles play from every tree
with rainbows of prisms sparkling free.
An awesome sight for all to see,
the sight that quietly beckons me.

A beauty only God could cast,
serenity while yet it lasts.
Not a mark on its unscarred face,
not a footprint can be traced.

Dare I disturb this quiet glow,
and plant my feet into the snow,
where my footprints will have marred
a mournful crunch into the yard?

But if I am to do my work,
I cannot my morning chores let shirk.
For in spite of the beauty that I see,
there are those that still depend on me.

A winter's day that God bequeathed,
another treasure He unleashed.
A memory I will tuck away,
the beauty of this, a winter's day.

Janice N. Chapman

The El Nino Children

*I can't remember a year quite like this
where opposite shores suffer El Nino's kiss.
Florida suffers while El Nino East cuts her path,
while California catches El Nino West's furious wrath.*

*She takes a bite of lovely shore,
and crunches pavements where roads once were.
Homes that beautifully were kept,
went down in gloom when El Nino swept.*

*Even the swamps and everglades caught her wrath
when El Nino East set out to cut her path.
While out west the coasts are snatched away,
and pavements are ripped from their highways.*

*The waves that sent these two to shore
have caused destruction and much, much more.
Neither in the East nor in the West is it safe to stay,
when the El Nino children come out to play.*

*Weather borned and nature spawned,
raised by violence, tribulation and brawn,
they compete along our shore lines and boast
that with destruction each has done the most.*

*They rage and slam and bury and claw,
their anger on our shores, unbridled and raw.
To us they give undying memories of fate,
these El Nino children of nineteen ninety-eight.*

Hello Out There

Hell's Highway

*They call it the Alcan —
that devilish stretch of "highway."
There's eighteen hundred miles
for which the Devil makes you pay.*

*Pot holes and chuck holes
the same beds are in —
and believe me when I tell you,
they were generous with all of them.*

*There are gullies I could hide my truck in,
gravel large enough to break my windshield, too;
A new paint job from the mud
that sticks to the sides of my truck like glue.*

*There are Pilot cars at the construction sites,
and the roads get narrow, if not a little bit tight.
If you have tires left when you come off that road,
they'll be "May pops" and ready to explode.*

*The bridges are narrow — only room for one — don't even
think two!
And the hairpin turns are plentiful and just waiting for you!
Your hair will stand up on the back of your neck, no doubt,and
you'll utter cuss words you thought you'd forgotten about.*

*Gas stations are few and far between.
Beats anything that I've ever seen.
Whatever thoughts you've ever had about Hell —
let them double, or triple, or at any rate, swell!*

*For once you get on the Alcan —
there's the Devil to pay. . .
Eighteen hundred slow, torturous, miles
of the Hell's Highway.*

The Glaciers

The glaciers stand out
from the mountain crests.
Each strutting the packed ice
it carries upon its chest.

Some are just babies
As glaciers go —
but give them a few hundred years,
and they'll grow.

And they'll be as big
as the big ones are now.
And the big ones will have moved
by the might of their ice somehow.

The rule of the thumb
the glaciers and mountains must apply,
"Hey, I'm bigger than you are —
Move over little guy!"

Hello Out There

A Farmer's Wife

A farmer's wife is really
a Jill of all trades.
She can do everything from dishes
To mending the pasture gates.
She's up early every morning,
no later than the crack of dawn.
She'll still be there long after dark,
and long after the sun is gone.

She'll be there in the cold
to help put out the cattle feed.
She'll plant a sizeable garden in the spring,
and most of it from seed.
She'll be there to help with harvest,
and take the dinners to the field,
when the sun is boiling down,
and the wheat is giving yield.
And when they come in from the fields in the evenings,
and he plops into a chair —

Guess who fixes meals and does the dishes,
and washes the baby's hair?
Guess who cans the vegetables they've grown,
and jellies the berries there,
and cans the fruits for them to eat
when winter next gets here.

He'll do the books and keep repaired
the machinery that he uses.
He keeps the barns in-tact, the fences mended,
and plenty of feed for cattle against the winter's ruses.
She gets little praise for her part
for all that she goes through,
to help him to be the one
the neighbors all look up to.

I'm a Meat and Potatoes Man

*I want all of you to know,
and to likewise understand,
I'm just an ordinary person,
but I'm a meat and potatoes man.*

*Everything I like to eat
can be grown right here on my own land.
Potatoes come from my own fields,
And beef from my own brand.*

*I may rise before daylight,
and my days may be hard and long,
But meat and potatoes will soothe my ache
even when my day goes wrong.*

*I don't want any fancy foods
placed upon my plate.
just good old meat and potatoes,
the rest will have to wait.*

*And when it comes my time
to lie beneath that hardened clay,
carved in that stone above
the hole in which I'll lay*

*I'd surely like to know
that my epitaph will say:
"He was a meat and potatoes man
to the end of his last day."*

Hello Out There

Grandpa's Garden

When Grandpa went out to till
the space for his garden site,
we all knew what was to come
would be a pure delight.

Beneath his loving care,
his tiller, spade and hoe,
it seemed to me that Grandpa
could make anything to grow.

He waited for the full of moon
to plant his beloved legumes.
Then he hoed and raked those awful weeds,
and sent them to their doom.

And once the ground warmed up,
and the dark of moon came around,
well, Grandpa would plant
his beloved tubers into the ground.

How good the turned earth smelled
to my uncanny nose
as I bent to help my Grandpa
plant those uneven rows.

And I marveled at the sight
that soon beneath the sun,
told me the rewards of
what Grandpa and me had done.

Those vines and bushes outdid themselves
To bear and bear and bear.
They all did us proud
beneath Grandpa's loving care.

And we all knew that anything else
Grandpa had to do would wait,
once he took up his spade and hoe
and went through that garden gate.

The Soil

I picked up a handful of soil,
and let it sift through my fingers.
I did this several times,
as at the edge of the field I lingered.

Soil freshly plowed has a fragrance
you can find no other place on earth.
And it reminds one of the Bible passage,
where from dust we were given birth.

And like persons who walk upon it,
rich in its own personal qualities,
poor in some areas, rich in others.
Clay or gumbo or sand it may be.

And yet it's a part of everything we do,
whether we plow it up, or build upon it,
drive upon it, or grow things in it,
or drink from the vessels made from it.

Where the grass grows upon it,
it's a full course dinner for those who reside,
and where it lines a water hole,
it squelches the thirst and cools the hide.

And as through my fingers the soil slides,
and the fine silt filters from it,
I breathe deeply of its fragrance.
I love the smell of it.

The Drought

The winter wore on
and the north winds blew.
I thought it might snow,
but no snowflakes flew.

The summer wore on
with no sign of rain,
and it seemed my best efforts
were only in vain.

The grass turned green;
and in a week turned brown.
And the cattle they died
where e're they laid down.

The idea seemed
somehow to be sane,
to sell my possessions
and move on again.

The buyer he laughed
as my face filled with pain,
and he bade me farewell
in a downpour of rain!

Hello Out There

Nature Things

The things I miss the most, I guess,
are all those things I loved the best.
The crimson glow of the setting sun
while evening chores were being done.
The croaking of an old bull frog.
The barking of the prairie dog.
The chirping crickets seemed so dear
while coyote chorus filled the air.
The coolness of the evening breeze
tickling the leaves of the gracious trees.
The hooting of an old hoot owl
when nightly varmints began to prowl.
The lowing of the cows, alas,
while bedding down on pasture grass.
Spring flowers lending their beauty to
the green pasture grasses and the dew.
The waving grains of golden wheat
waving gently in the summer heat.
As though a blessing from above
All those things I learned to love.
If I could I'd drink a toast
to all those things that Nature hosts.

Janice N. Chapman

Love

Hello Out There

It Couldn't Be

Through the tears and heartache
She understood me not —
Assured me that very soon
my woes would be forgot.

That I would someday thank her,
for all that she had done,
to help me to realize
the battle had been won.

That I would someday find
a love by far more true,
and know that in the past
she had seen me through.

That she had always loved me
and done the best she could,
to raise me knowing right from wrong
and to forgive her, as I should.

But though the years go passing by,
and I love her as I can,
deep inside I wonder —
will she ever understand

that the love I felt for him,
and his promises of love,
were blessings bestowed upon us
from our Father up above?

One Heart for Sale

I've got one heart for sale,
it's broken.
It's all that he left
for a token.

The pieces are shattered,
I can't find them.
They're all that he left
behind him.

Would you want a heart?
It's unique.
It's broken, but then,
it's an antique.

I'll never forget him,
I know.
But I hope my feelings
don't show.

Would you want a heart
that's broken?
Would you want an
ex-love's token?

Hello Out There

Eight Track Tape

*You are just like an eight track tape
in everything you do.
When side one is all played out,
you flip over to side two.*

*You say I don't know you,
and I don't know what you do.
And you don't know how sometimes
I wish those words were true!*

*On track one I hear your sorry's
when you've ran out of lies.
Track two asks my forgiveness
for those outrageous alibies.*

*Track three tells of all the ways
you have used your many charms,
to lure all of those lovely creatures
into your lonely, loving arms.*

*Track four wails of your love affairs
and all that you've gone through.
And no one else can tell it
and make it sound the way you do!*

*Track five is fill with deception
and the blame is all on me.
I shouldn't see and hear
all those things I hear and see.*

Track six is contradiction

*of the things you say you do,
and filled with all the secrets
I shouldn't know about you.*

*Track seven is a no win situation,
where there's no way I can win.
I keep listening to your lies,
and I keep taking you back again.*

*Track eight leaves you blameless,
you can't help it that you're a fan.
It's a flaw within your make up,
that you're a ladies' man.*

*But your habits run a pattern
that has caused our love to die.
And I can't even find the tears
that it would take for me to cry.*

*If you're leaving me again,
don't bother to come back.
Find someone else to fall for
your life as an eight Track.*

Hello Out There

Your Game of Hearts

*You've used every heart that has fallen for you;
abused it, misused it, and left it for a new.
You've broken more hearts than anyone I ever knew,
and a heartbreak is something for which a body can't sue.*

*A computer machine would be put to shame
by the things that you've done to win your way to fame.
You're filled with the charm anyone's heart to tame,
but woe to the heart on which you stake your claim!*

*Like a dealer who deals out a new deck of cards,
you deal out each hand without any regards
to the stakes that may follow the game as it's played,
because the dealer will be the only one who has stayed.*

*You break in new hearts by ones and by twos;
it bothers you not, you've got nothing to lose.
I feel for you, mister, and all of your kind.
You'd ruin a good heart just to have a good time.*

*When you finally wake up in the future at last,
and look back through the hearts you have left in the past,
I've got news for you, mister, you won't like the cost,
the day you wake up and realize just what you have lost.*

The Man for Whom She Cries

Sit back and let me tell you
a story of a friend of mine.
She fell so much in love
that she was completely blind.

She thought so much of him,
his faults she never seen.
And he thought it was so cute
to let this woman dream.

Not once did he correct her
that his feelings for her weren't there,
or that never during her living years
would his love she ever share.

She let herself be both faithful and loyal,
loving always the man she saw in him,
Never dreaming as she continued to love,
he would break her heart in the end.

Though he posed as such a gentleman,
and treated her like a lady, too.
And she trusted and believed in him,
this man she'd given her heart to.

And when he came by one night
to tell her to leave him alone,
He may as well have killed her,
as to have left her there to atone.

For the emptiness she carries with her now,

Hello Out There

and the tears she cries each night,
cannot erase the hollowness,
nor turn her world back right.

For she could not have guessed
the man for whom she fell,
would cause her pain in the end,
and put her down through hell.

For she was just a plaything,
though she knew it not back then.
Nor did she know the cruelty inside
this man she'd called a friend.

She could not know his ruthlessness
when she first fell in love.
And it seemed that only laughter was what she got
from both him and God above.

For her prayers seemed to have gone unanswered,
And the man who had never cared,
knows not her every thought was for his happiness,
and the love she thought she shared.

And it's a heavy cross to have to bear,
that the man for whom she cries,
would accept from her a love so beautiful,
and belittle her with his lies.

Janice N. Chapman

Uncle Sam's G. I.

You asked me how long I'll be here. . .
Well, honey, that's something I don't know.
I'll be here until Uncle Sam gives me orders,
and then like all the rest I'll pack and go.

So let's enjoy the time we have together.
Let's make some memories while we have time.
And if we should need to cry on someone's shoulder,
I'll cry on yours, and you can cry on mine.

Let's be friends and let's have our fun.
We'll bowl and dance and dine and do the town.
We'll go out and see all that we can see,
and be the fun lovin'est couple in this town.

And when it comes time for me to be leaving,
I don't want to see a single tear in your eye.
Smile and kiss me and wish me luck and remember,
I'm a serviceman — an Uncle Sam's G. I..

But don't get any ideas about romance.
That's a thing that's not for you and me.
Because when I get my orders to leave this post,
I don't want to know you've cried for me.

Because when I leave, honey, I'll be forgetting
all of the places where I've just been.
But while I'm here I'll do my darnedest
to enjoy the best of everything in them.

You'll be the kind of girl I'll be looking for,

*if I should decide to ever settle down.
But there's no telling how long it will be
until that future time rolls around.*

*So, I'll just consider you a lucky girl,
and call myself one darn lucky guy...
And the both of us together will remember,
I'm a serviceman — an Uncle Sam's G. I..*

Love Library

*You tell me you love me,
but how long will it be
until my love goes on the shelves
of your love library?*

*How many memories do you have
among the volumes there,
of all the girls who fell for you
and thought you really cared?*

*How many different kinds of love
do the chapters there contain,
in memory of the girls who've gave
their love to you in vain?*

*The books in your love library
you're writing just for you,
to look back on in your old age
upon the things you used to do.*

*And if I were to look me up
tonight after you have gone,
on what page of what volume
would I find myself on?*

Hello Out There

Old Souvenirs

I surprised myself today while throwing things away.
Found a box packed full of things from yesterday.
I found myself fighting back some tears
as I sorted through the memories of yesteryears.

There's the little card that made me a slave
to your sweet tender words and your aftershave.
In its own little box, a string of pearls —
just like the ones you gave to all the girls.

An old class ring and a letter jacket, too.
A stack of old love letters signed, "I love you."
A bunch of small trinkets from the summer fair,
and a Japanese fan you'd sent from over there.

The roses I'd pressed in a book you'd gave,
and photographs galore I had chosen to save.
A small bottle of perfume still partially used,
a gift you knew I couldn't refuse.

I couldn't bring myself to throw away
those old memories from yesterday.
Old souvenirs from the years long gone by. . .
In their own little box in my attic they lie.

Janice N. Chapman

The Angel Was Crying

*I saw an angel, she was crying last night.
The tears spilled down over her robe of white.
But as it sometimes will happen that way,
her death had robbed her of her wedding day.*

*She lives in Heaven with angels galore,
but she longs for the arms that hold her no more.
To be back here with the one she adores,
she'd trade her halo and the wings that she wore.*

*We think of Heaven as something that's good.
But the angel was crying, and from what I understood,
she'd give up Heaven, its glory and its fame,
for the honor of wearing her sweetheart's name.*

*They knew a love that few of us know;
a rare kind of love that continues to grow,
like a flower that blossoms beneath the sun,
and knows no end to the beauty it's spun.*

*While we think of Heaven and its happiness,
The angel was crying in her loneliness.
She can't be happy on Heaven's bright shore
until her beloved is with her once more.*

Hello Out There

Thank You for Sharing My Life

I can't say I love you — but I do.
I can't live my life with you — but I will.
I can't put my arms around you —but I have.
I can't kiss those tender lips — and feel the thrill.
I can live with the memories — and the dreams.
I've spent years loving you — or so it seems.
I can remember the good times — we had together.
I can't feel shame for — anything.
Loving you must have been the best thing — I have ever done.
It taught me to be a woman — not a child on the run.
I know I won't forget you — any more than you will me.
But I can still feel grateful — for having you love me.
And while your children call you — Daddy.
And while you call their mother — your wife.
I can still say thank you — Thank you .
Thank you for sharing my life.